# Mr. HAPPY

## presents
## Dillydale Day

### ...and other stories

**EGMONT**
*We bring stories to life*

First published in Great Britain 2009 by Egmont UK Limited
239 Kensington High Street, London W8 6SA
Copyright © 2009 THOIP (a Chorion company). All rights reserved.
THE MR. MEN SHOW™ and DILLYDALE™ are trademarks
of THOIP (a Chorion company). All rights reserved.

ISBN 978 1 4052 4682 8
1 3 5 7 9 10 8 6 4 2
Printed in Malaysia

It's an exciting day in Dillydale. Even more exciting than usual. It's that special day when friends and neighbours come together to create the biggest party of the year!

Let's get the party started by playing a Dillydale Day game. Find the matching stickers to the scenes below, then find three differences between the matching images.

**1**

**Stick your sticker here!**

**2**

**Stick your sticker here!**

Answers: 1. The bucket Mr Bounce is standing in has changed colour, part of the lamp is missing and there is a cloud missing. 2. Miss Naughty's nose is a different colour, a green balloon is missing and the flag on the tent has changed colour.

# Mr Happy
## Presents Dillydale Day

Mr Happy is very excited to be presenting the most important day in the Dillydale calendar. Let's just hope it goes off without too many glitches.

"Testing, one, two," beams Mr Happy. "What a turnout to celebrate Dillydale Day, the happiest day of the whole year."

"So, that's why everybody is here," frowns Mr Scatterbrain. "Silly me. I thought it was a festival of sponges."

Sorry, fellas!

"It's a Dillydale Day celebration! To help us kick things off is our special musical guest, Little Miss Chatterbox!" grins Mr Happy.

Miss Chatterbox takes to the stage with a rather creaky guitar.
"It's so great to be here!" cries Miss Chatterbox. "I'd like to play something especially for Dillydale Day. Well, actually, I wrote it for my garden gnome, who just loves my music. I hope you will, too. Here goes, Dillydale . . ."

But something doesn't sound quite right. As Miss Chatterbox strums her guitar, one of the strings pops off. It pings through the air and wallops Mr Bump right on his back!

Poopity Poop!

Miss Chatterbox tries to tune her other strings but before she can sing a note, another string snaps and hurtles through the air at great speed.

This time Mr Bump is ready with a plate cunningly disguised as a shield.

Not this time, you evil string!

But it's no use. Even the shield can't protect Mr Bump. Before another string can escape from the guitar, Mr Bump flees to safety.

Well, so much for my guitar. Just as well I can play the accordion. I do hope you all like the sound of my accordian, not everyone enjoys the complicated sound, apart from my gnome maybe. But I am sure you will all agree, it is rather pretty!

The rusty accordion screeches into action, piercing the air with an earsplitting sound. Soon, the Mr Men and Little Misses run for cover and the first musical event of Dillydale Day is over. Phew!

Ah, those colourful posters can mean only one thing. The circus has come to Dillydale! Why don't you create your own Mr Men circus poster? Use your stickers to make it as fun as you can!

# Little Miss Chatterbox's
## Ring of Mayhem

The citizens of Dillydale better hold on to their hats as Miss Chatterbox takes her place in the circus ring.

Welcome to the circus! I'm your ringmaster, Miss Chatterbox! Wow, I've always wanted to say that. I've dreamed of being a ringmaster even longer than I've dreamed of being an astronaut. But I thought both were really, really hard jobs, so that's why I took up knitting . . .

Before Miss Chatterbox can utter another word, Mr Bump takes his place in ring one. He perches on a peculiar green stallion called Rex. Mr Bump isn't looking so confident.

Things start off well for our bumpy friend. Mr Bump is soon racing around the ring faster than Miss Chatterbox can talk. And that is seriously fast! But nothing runs smoothly in Dillydale and it is not long before Mr Bump hits some trouble and flies off his stallion . . .

. . . but Miss Chatterbox is so busy talking, she doesn't notice a thing!

On with the next part of the show! Oh, I love this part. Mr Bounce is now going to leap off the top of the ladder and land in a teeny-weeny little bucket of water!

Mr Bounce is feeling nervous. The ladder is very, very high.

Mr Bounce weighs up the stunt. He needs complete silence.

It's a difficult trick. Ssh, ssh, ssh, audience. Please be very quiet. Mr Bounce must concentrate on landing on the exact spot. Nobody must say a word. Not a single word, otherwise he could miss the bucket and that wouldn't be very good, would it?

As Mr Bounce hurtles through the air, Miss Chatterbox cannot help but chatter. With every word she utters, Mr Bounce gets more and more and more distracted.

Until he can no longer see the bucket and lands on the ground.

Uh-oh! Whee! Goodbye!

He doesn't bounce far before he finds trouble in the shape of Mr Bump and a certain green stallion.

Miss Chatterbox is so busy talking, she doesn't notice a thing!

Oh goodness, is it time for Little Miss Calamity's act already? May I direct your attention to the centre of the ring, where Miss Calamity is going to ride a bicycle across a tightrope. Blindfolded!

Miss Calamity is afraid. Her bike is rather wobbly. And the rope is very thin. She needs ultimate silence if she is going to make it.

She starts well. Not a sound can be heard as she races towards the crucial midway point.

That is until a certain somebody opens their mouth.

OH MY GOSH! Miss Calamity's going to make it! What a star . . .

Miss Chatterbox's words bounce around the circus tent.
Miss Calamity loses concentration and topples off her tightrope!

What a calamity!

Aaaaarrgghhh!

Miss Calamity heads straight for Rex and lands with a bump! Taking no more chances in Miss Chatterbox's circus tent, Rex bolts out of the door with the three Dillydalers hanging on for dear life!

And so, the circus draws to an end. Who knows where Miss Calamity, Mr Bounce and Mr Bump will end up, but just remember to take extra care should a certain Miss Chatterbox lead a circus near you . . .

The country fair, a place where the Dillydalers freely mingle with farm animals and show off their prize-winning vegetables.

Help Mr Nervous find the wiggly path to Little Miss Sunshine before Little Miss Scary's prize bull catches up with him!

# Mr Pernickety
## and the Greased Pig

It's the most popular event of the fair, the greased pig-catching competition. Only one fussy citizen of Dillydale is not quite so convinced.

"Explain to me again, Little Miss Naughty," begins Mr Pernickety, "why would anyone want to volunteer to catch a greased pig?"

"I think it looks like so much fun!" giggles Miss Naughty.

"Fun, Miss Naughty, is organising your sock drawer, not rolling in muck," frowns Mr Pernickety.

Suddenly, a dollop of slimy mud flies from the pit and splats Mr Pernickety's bow tie.

How revolting!

Mr Pernickety decides that enough is enough and there are far more important things to attend to, but before he has a chance to leave, Mr Happy gets ready to make an important announcement.

Our next contestant is . . . Mr Pernickety!

Mr Pernickety marches right up to Mr Happy to protest, but Mr Happy pulls out a competition card with Mr Pernickety's name written in bold black ink.

This must be a mistake!

The handwriting looks a little familiar. Then Mr Pernickety hears a loud cackle coming from the side of the ring.

I signed you up! Sometimes I just can't help myself!

Miss Naughty is laughing so loudly, Mr Pernickety cannot ignore her for another second.

Before Mr Pernickety has time to reply, Mr Tickle drags him into the ring.

"Come on down, Mr Pernickety. The whole fair is waiting," grins Mr Tickle. "There's no turning back now!"

Mr Pernickety tries to escape but Mr Tickle is fast and pulls him back into the ring.

Whether Mr Pernickety likes it or not, it looks like he has a greased pig to catch!

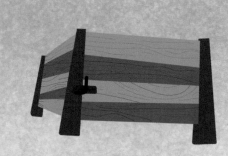

The shed, holding the pig in the corner of the pen, starts to rumble. And shake. Whatever is waiting for Mr Pernickety must be HUGE!

Suddenly, the shed bursts open and out runs the biggest pig Dillydale has ever seen!

CRASH!

He soon runs into trouble when he hits a pile of mud in the ring. With the most pernickety of care, he dashes in and out of the mud, like a ballerina.

There's only one thing for it. Mr Pernickety tries to climb over the fence to escape the rotten pig, once and for all.

Mr Pernickety runs as quickly as his fussy little legs will carry him.

Even Mr Pernickety can't keep his bow tie clean forever though, and it's not long before he finds himself taking a rather graceless dive into the slimy mud.

Save these stickers for
'Lost and Found' and
'Wheel of Mayhem'
on pages 28 and 29.

Somebody needs a tickle!

Use these stickers for your sketch show on pages 30 and 31!

And these are just for fun!

Things don't go quite to plan. With a huge crash, the greased pig is soon carrying Mr Pernickety around and around the ring at rocket speed!

Let's hear it for Mr Pernickety! He's just set a new Dillydale record!

After twenty-two nail biting circuits of the ring, the greased pig finally slows to a stop. Mr Pernickety slides down the slimy pig.

You were great!

Mr Pernickety wipes the mud from his hair and collects his trophy. There is just one person that he needs to deal with.

"If it weren't for this lovely trophy, I would be quite cross with you," Mr Pernickety begins. "But it is a very shiny trophy, so I forgive you."

"Great!" giggles Miss Naughty. "I've signed you up for bull fighting next!"

I think I'm going to faint!

The Mr Men and Little Misses have gathered to watch the movie trailer of the year, 'Gamma Goo from Planet Nine'! Two Dillydalers are late. Use the clues below to work out who they are.

When you've worked it out, find the stickers of the missing friends and put them in their seats before the movie begins . . .

Missing Dillydaler 1: He is never far from his bandages!
Missing Dillydaler 2: This tiny friend wears an extra long top hat!

18

# Gamma Goo
## from Planet Nine

It came without warning. Nobody knows from where. But it's here, and there is no way to stop it! It's 'Gamma Goo from Planet Nine'!

Starring Little Miss Sunshine as Victoria Wellbeloved!

The nanny who was the first to see the horror unleashed by the goo!

And starring Mr Bump as Captain Raphe Daniels. The only man brave enough to battle the unyielding slime.

I'll stop you, goo! If it's the last thing I do!

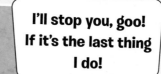

But time is running out. The city is under siege.

19

It's man against monster in a battle to save the city from this oozing enemy.

No one can escape the slime.
Not even Victoria.
Or can she?

Save yourself!
It's too late for me!

I'm not leaving you behind, Victoria!

Captain Raphe's super-slime-freezer gun soon freezes the goo and Victoria is safe! For now . . .

It takes a team to eliminate this seeping, creeping wall of goo. And they do it, but to make sure it never happens again our heroes must take on the devious alien behind the deadly slime . . .

DEMENTICON! Brilliantly played by the talented, Little Miss Scary.

But things are only just beginning.

My slime will rule the world!

STOP! In the name of Raphe!

To be continued . . .

Whatever you do, don't miss 'Gamma Goo from Planet Nine', coming to a Dillydale cinema near you!

The amusement park - one of the most thrilling places on Earth. And if it's an amusement park in Dillydale, then there is no end to the thrills it brings. Use your stickers to bring the amusement park to life!

# Little Miss Whoops
## and the Toffee Apple

Miss Whoops is very excited to be working on the Ferris wheel. First stop is to secure Mr Grumpy and Mr Tickle into their seats. After all, who knows what could happen on a ride controlled by Dillydale's clumsiest resident!

"I didn't know you worked here," growls Mr Grumpy.
"It's only my second day," replies Miss Whoops. "But let me tell you, Mr Grumpy, I'm really starting to get the hang of it!"

Let's just hope Miss Whoops can concentrate on her new job. After all, that toffee apple does look rather distracting.

Mmmm . . . delicious!

23

"I really love Ferris wheels," giggles Mr Tickle. "Don't you, Mr Grumpy?"
"Um, let me think," grumbles Mr Grumpy. "No."

But it's too late for Mr Grumpy to jump off now, as the big wheel creaks into motion.

I know a grumpy grape who needs a tickle!

"I wouldn't if I were you," booms Mr Grumpy. "It's a long way down."

Mr Tickle does what he is told. They certainly are very high up.

Two carriages along, Mr Strong and Mr Bounce are circling high above Dillydale.

Boy, are we high!

Good thing we have this safety bar!

Before they have a chance to utter another word, Mr Strong pulls the safety bar from its hinges.

At least Mr Nervous and Miss Scary are behaving themselves. Or are they?

Oh, pickles!

"Ha ha! Watch out, Mr Nervous. Don't fall out!" screams Miss Scary. "Oh, but look at that loose bolt!"

"No, no, no. Don't do that. Please don't do that," whimpers Mr Nervous. "No, no, can't hold on . . ."

Back on the ground, Miss Whoops is busy gobbling her toffee apple.

Mmm! Just one more lick!

It tastes so delicious that she forgets all about her job. When she turns around, her toffee apple sticks to the controls with a big fat SLURP!

The toffee apple pushes down the acceleration lever. It's not long before the Dillydale citizens are hurtling around and around the Ferris wheel at top speed.

Without his safety bar, Mr Bounce cannot hold on for a second longer. He bounces out of the carriage and away from the speeding wheel.

Is it me or are we going faster?

Wheeeee!

I feel very dizzy, Mr Grumpy!

Whoops!

SNAP!

Down below, Miss Whoops is not having much luck trying to slow down the Ferris wheel. In fact, things suddenly get worse when the emergency handbrake snaps in two!

By now, the Dillydale heroes are racing round the wheel so fast, they are starting to see double.

As Mr Nervous approaches the bottom, he tries to make a bid for freedom. But it's no use. "Let's go round again!" screams Miss Scary. "Faster! Faster!"

And so the Dillydale friends set off on another knuckle biting ride on the Ferris wheel. And what of Miss Whoops? Well, she is far too busy rescuing her yummy toffee apple to notice a thing!

# Lost and Found

Mr Rude has hidden some of Mr Scatterbrain's belongings, making Mr Scatterbrain even more confused! Can you find where the objects are hidden? Look high, look low, leave no Dillydaler unturned! When you've found them, place the matching sticker over the hidden object so Mr Scatterbrain can find them again.

**Things to find:**

Sandwich
Phone
Ketchup
Banjo

Answers: Mr Small is holding the sandwich, Little Miss Sunshine has the mobile phone, the ketchup is beside Little Miss Calamity and Mr Rude is hiding the banjo.

# Wheel of Mayhem

Are you ready to make the Mr Men Wheel of Mayhem? Just answer the questions below about your favourite Dillydalers, find the correct sticker and stick it in the wheel until it is filled with colour and calamity!

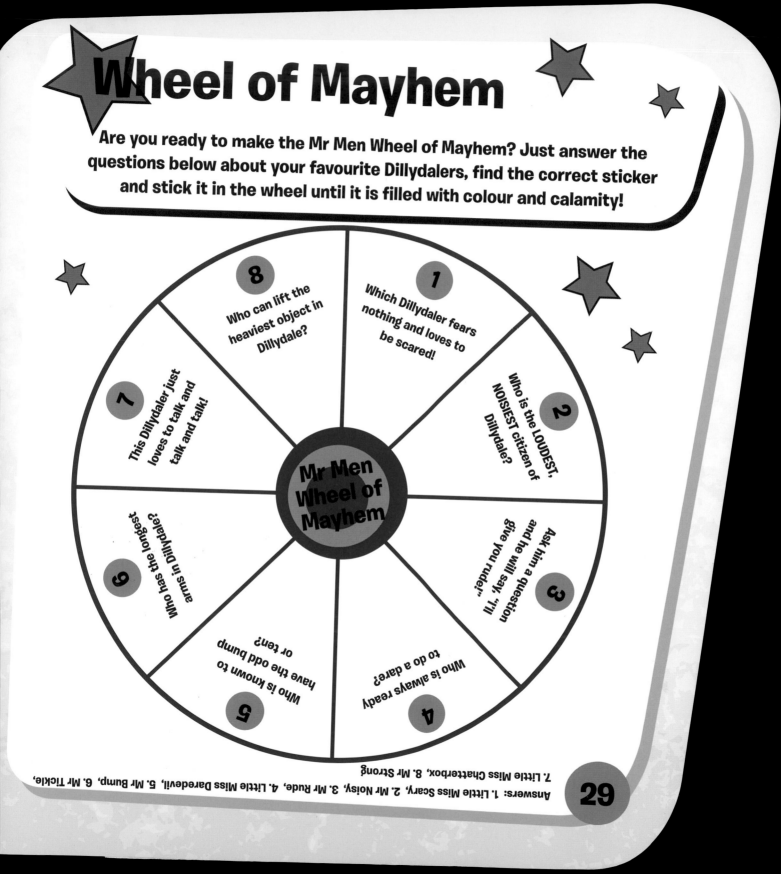

**8** Who can lift the heaviest object in Dillydale?

**1** Which Dillydaler fears nothing and loves to be scared!

**2** Who is the LOUDEST, NOISIEST citizen of Dillydale?

**7** This Dillydaler just loves to talk and talk and talk!

**Mr Men Wheel of Mayhem**

**3** Ask him a question and he will say, "I'll give you rude!"

**6** Who has the longest arms in Dillydale?

**5** Who is known to have the odd bump or ten?

**4** Who is always ready to do a dare?

Answers: 1. Little Miss Scary, 2. Mr Noisy, 3. Mr Rude, 4. Little Miss Daredevil, 5. Mr Bump, 6. Mr Tickle, 7. Little Miss Chatterbox, 8. Mr Strong.

29

# The Circus Crusade

Now it's your turn to create some pictures! Complete the scenes with your stickers, using the story to help you. There are some speech bubble stickers that you can add to make it extra fun!

It is circus time in Dillydale and the Mr Men and Little Misses are very busy. Mr Tickle is practising his accordion, only it sounds out of tune. Mr Grumpy is riding a rather strange bicycle but he doesn't seem very happy. And Mr Small looks very tall, but also very wobbly, on his super stilts for one.

It is not long before the circus sets off with a crash, bang, wallop and things soon get out of hand. Mr Scatterbrain throws a banana pie at Mr Pernickety. Then Mr Tickle tickles Mr Grumpy until he falls off his bicycle and falls flat on to the floor!

Suddenly, the tent poles come loose and the tent crashes to the ground! One by one, the Dillydalers whiz down the tent to safety. "This is the best ride ever!" shouts Little Miss Daredevil.
And so, here we leave the Mr Men and Little Misses, sliding down their broken circus tent, in true Dillydale style! Until next year . . .

The End

32